BIRDS™
IDW
PACHECO
ANGRY BIRDS
COMICS
FLY OFF THE HANDLE

Cover Artwork by: Ciro Cangialosi

Edited for IDW by: David Hedgecock
Collection Edits by: Justin Eisinger & Alonzo Simon
Collection Production by: Chris Mowry
Publisher: Ted Adams

KAIKEN
PUBLISHING LTD.

Laura Nevanlinna, Publishing Director
Jukka Heiskanen, Editor-in-Chief, Comics
Juha Mäkinen, Editor, Comics
Jan Schulte-Tigges, Art Director, Comics
Henri Sarimo, Graphic Designer
Nathan Cosby, Freelance Editor

ROVIO

Thanks to Jukka Heiskanen, Juha Mäkinen, and the Kaiken team for their hard work and invaluable assistance.

ISBN: 978-1-63140-653-9

19 18 17 16 2 3 4 5

IDW
www.IDWPUBLISHING.com

Ted Adams, CEO & Publisher
Greg Goldstein, President & COO
Robbie Robbins, EVP/Sr. Graphic Artist
Chris Ryall, Chief Creative Officer/Editor-in-Chief
Matthew Ruzicka, CPA, Chief Financial Officer
Dirk Wood, VP of Marketing
Lorelei Bunjes, VP of Digital Services
Jeff Webber, VP of Licensing, Digital and Subsidiary Rights
Jerry Bennington, VP of New Product Development

Facebook: facebook.com/idwpublishing
Twitter: @idwpublishing
YouTube: youtube.com/idwpublishing
Tumblr: tumblr.idwpublishing.com
Instagram: instagram.com/idwpublishing

NGRY BIRDX

AB 2013-067

ORNING ON PIGGY ISLAND.

ZZZZZZZ

HMMM?

SUNRISE?

YAAAAWN

Written by: Paul Tobin • **Art by:** Paco Rodriques • **Colors by:** Digikore • **Letters by:** Pisara Oy

AHHH, HOW ***REFRESHING.*** IT'S ANOTHER ***BEAUTIFUL MORNING.***

A QUICK SHOWER, AND THEN IT'S TIME TO START THE DAY.

I WONDER WHERE THE ***OTHER*** BIRDS ARE.

BOUND

BOUND

BOUND

CHUCK?

MATILDA?

BOMB?

HMMM. USUALLY I CAN ***AT LEAST*** HEAR THE ***BOYS*** PLAYING.

OR ***DESTROYING SOMETHING.***

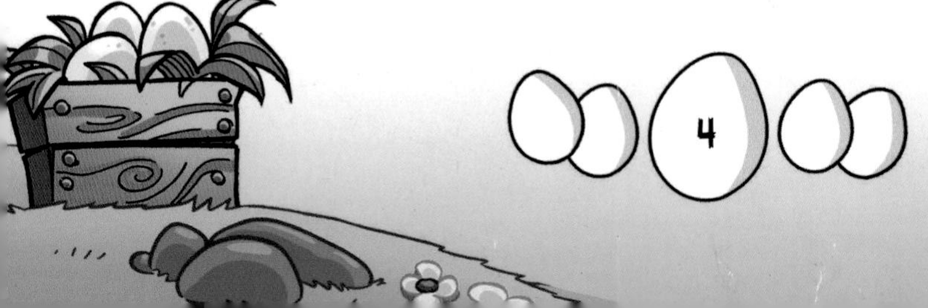

THE *EGGS* ARE SAFE, BUT...

...WHERE *IS* EVERYONE?

ARE THEY PRACTICING WITH THE *SLINGSHOTS?*

POOH!

HMMM. *DUSTY.* NO ONE'S BEEN HERE IN A WHILE.

HELLO?

HELLO?

HELLO?

SOUTH BEACH...
HELLO?
SQUARE FOREST...
HELLO?
THE COBALT PLATEAUS...
HELLO?
THE CROWN MOUNTAINS
ANYBODY?
THE BAMBOO FOREST.
HELLO? HELLO?
WHERE IS EVERY-ONE?!!!

I'M... ALONE?
COULD THEY HAVE FALLEN DOWN A HOLE?
BEEN SWEPT OUT TO SEA?
CAUGHT IN AN AVALANCHE?
OR... WAIT A SECOND...

THE PIGS!
SOON, AT THE GATES...
RUMBLE
RUMBLE
RUMBLE
RUMBLE
RUMBLE
?
!
HALT!
OR... NOT.

WHERE ARE THEY?
WHAT HAVE YOU DONE WITH THEM?
THOOP!
THOOP!
SPLONNG!
GRRRRR.
WE DON'T HAVE THE EGGS!
I PROMISE!
I PROMISE TWICE!
I'M NOT TALKING ABOUT THE EGGS!
NO EGGS! I PROMISE THAT I PROMISE!
WHERE ARE THE BIRDS?
WHERE ARE MY FRIENDS?
WHAKK!
WHAKK!
SMAKK!
ARE THEY IN HERE?!!
CRASSSHHH
YAHHH!
KEE-RASSSHHHHH!
???

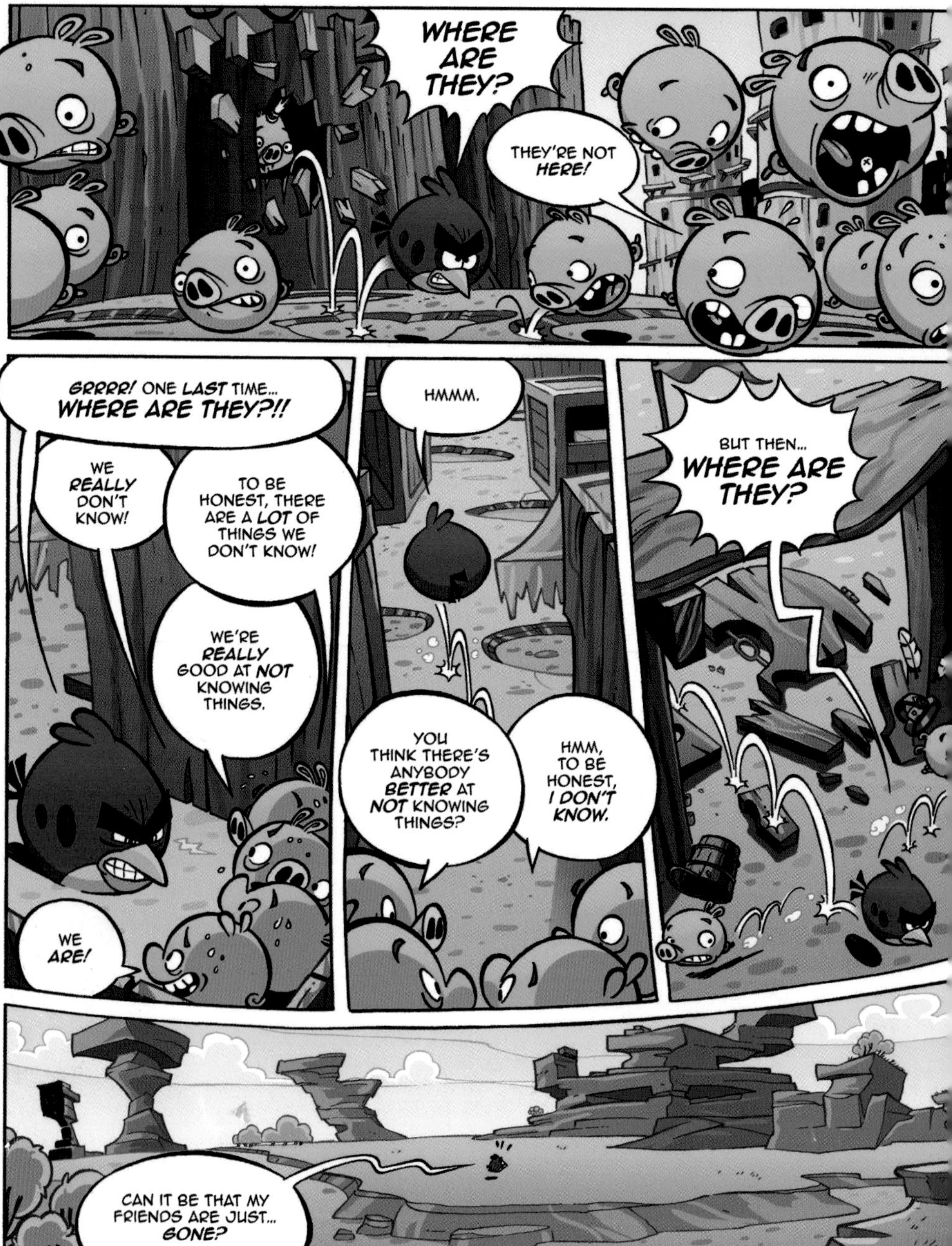

WHERE ARE THEY?

THEY'RE NOT *HERE!*

GRRRR! ONE *LAST* TIME... **WHERE ARE THEY?!!**

WE *REALLY* DON'T KNOW!

TO BE HONEST, THERE ARE A *LOT* OF THINGS WE DON'T KNOW!

WE'RE *REALLY* GOOD AT *NOT* KNOWING THINGS.

WE *ARE!*

HMMM.

YOU THINK THERE'S ANYBODY *BETTER* AT *NOT* KNOWING THINGS?

HMM, TO BE HONEST, *I DON'T KNOW.*

BUT THEN... **WHERE ARE THEY?**

CAN IT BE THAT MY FRIENDS ARE JUST... *GONE?*

AM I...
ALONE?
SNIFF
SHUFFLE!
?
HUH?
SHUFFLE!

SURPRISE!
AHHHHH!
HAPPY BIRTHDAY, RED!
CHUCK! BOMB! MATILDA! JAY! JIM! JAKE! TERENCE! WHERE HAVE YOU ALL BEEN?
WE'VE BEEN IN HIDING!
PLANNING YOUR SURPRISE PARTY!
WHY? DID YOU GET LONELY?
HUH?
ME?
LONELY?
NEVER.
SNIFF
THE END.

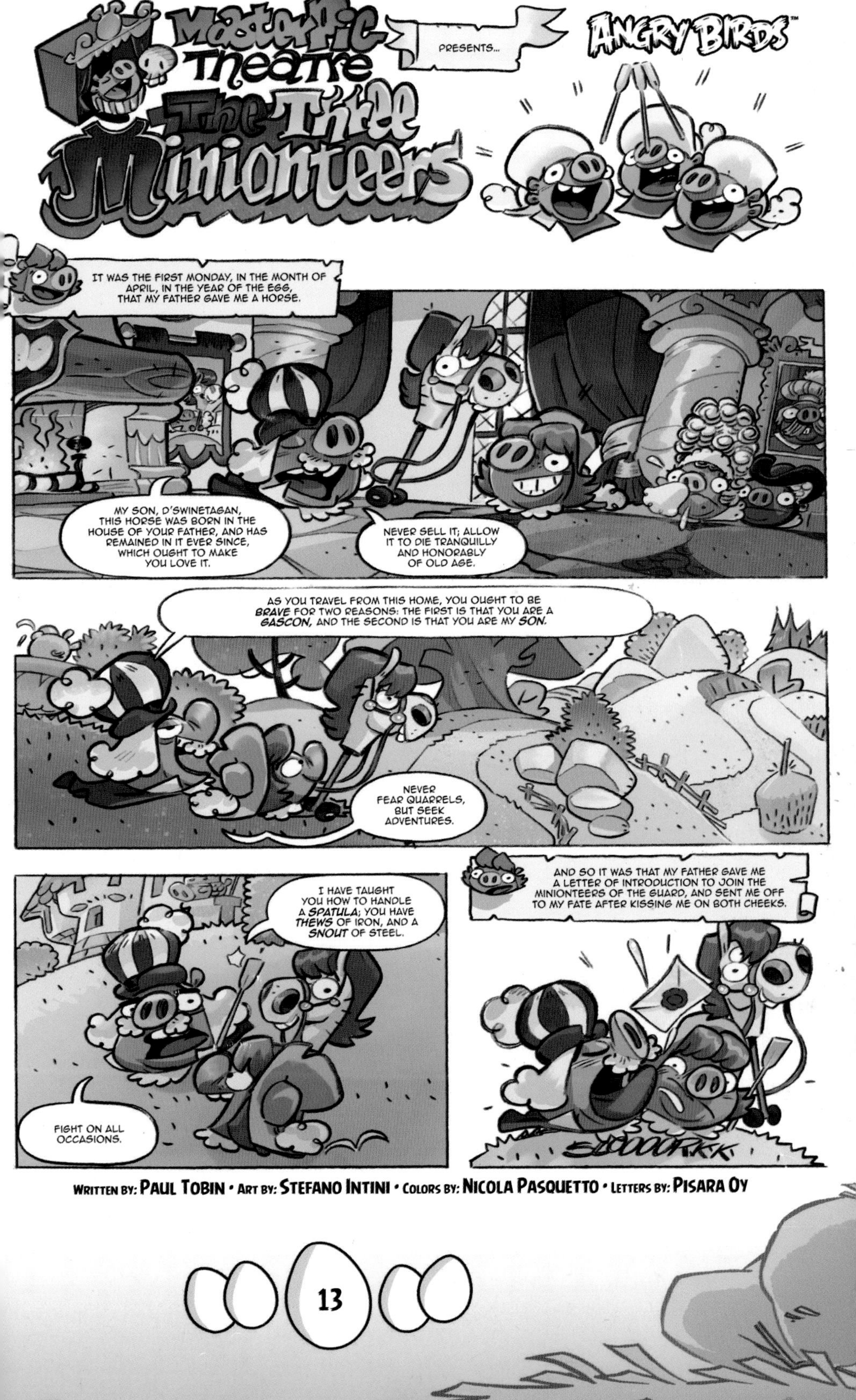

Masterpig Theatre
PRESENTS...
ANGRY BIRDS™
The Three Minionteers
IT WAS THE FIRST MONDAY, IN THE MONTH OF APRIL, IN THE YEAR OF THE EGG, THAT MY FATHER GAVE ME A HORSE.
MY SON, D'SWINETAGAN, THIS HORSE WAS BORN IN THE HOUSE OF YOUR FATHER, AND HAS REMAINED IN IT EVER SINCE, WHICH OUGHT TO MAKE YOU LOVE IT.
NEVER SELL IT; ALLOW IT TO DIE TRANQUILLY AND HONORABLY OF OLD AGE.
AS YOU TRAVEL FROM THIS HOME, YOU OUGHT TO BE BRAVE FOR TWO REASONS: THE FIRST IS THAT YOU ARE A GASCON, AND THE SECOND IS THAT YOU ARE MY SON.
NEVER FEAR QUARRELS, BUT SEEK ADVENTURES.
I HAVE TAUGHT YOU HOW TO HANDLE A SPATULA; YOU HAVE THEWS OF IRON, AND A SNOUT OF STEEL.
FIGHT ON ALL OCCASIONS.
AND SO IT WAS THAT MY FATHER GAVE ME A LETTER OF INTRODUCTION TO JOIN THE MINIONTEERS OF THE GUARD, AND SENT ME OFF TO MY FATE AFTER KISSING ME ON BOTH CHEEKS.
SLOOOORKK

WRITTEN BY: PAUL TOBIN • ART BY: STEFANO INTINI • COLORS BY: NICOLA PASQUETTO • LETTERS BY: PISARA OY

I SET OFF FOR PARIS WITH A HEART YEARNING FOR ADVENTURE AND THE COMPANIONSHIP OF MY GOOD HORSE, CLYDE.
CLOP
CLOP
CLOP
PARIS
FIGHT SCENE
YOU CAN IMAGINE, THEN, THE RAGE INSTILLED IN MY HEART WHEN, STOPPING AT A LOCAL TROUGH, I OVERHEARD A POMPOUS AND IMPERTINENT PERSONAGE MAKING FUN OF MY NOBLE FAMILY STEED.
THIS HORSE IS A PIMPLE! A TOAD! I'VE SEEN NOSTRIL HAIRS WITH MORE NOBILITY.
CAFE 'O
HA HA HA
THE BIRD HAD BLACK AND PIERCING EYES, A RED COMPLEXION, A STRONGLY MARKED BEAK, AND A BLACK AND WELL-SHAPED MUSTACHE. I DISLIKED HIM AT ONCE, AND EVEN AT TWICE.
I HAD NO CHOICE BUT TO CHALLENGE THIS MAN TO A DUEL.
I CHALLENGE YOU!
CHALLENGE HIM CHALLENGE HIM CHALLENGE HIM
AND SO WE FOUGHT! FLASHING SPATULAS! THE CHAOS OF BATTLE! THE VERY PULSE OF ADVENTURE!

THE BATTLE LASTED TWO SECONDS. I WAS SOUNDLY BEATEN. AND MY LETTER OF INTRODUCTION WAS STOLEN.
HA HA HA HA-HA HA
ADVENTURING IS HARD WORK, CLYDE.
AND SO IT WAS THAT I RODE INTO PARIS IN DISGRACE.
LOOK MOMMY, A DISGRACE!
WITHOUT MY LETTER OF INTRODUCTION, I WAS REFUSED ENTRY INTO THE MINIONTEERS.
I REFUSE!
AND IT WAS THEN THAT I SAW, FROM A WINDOW, THE VERY BIRD WHO HAD BESTED ME IN COMBAT! A BIRD KNOWN AS...

CARDINAL CARDINALIEU!
WAIT! I WANT TO MAKE COMBAT WITH YOU AGAIN, YOU FOUL FOWL!
BUT AS CHANCE WOULD HAVE IT, IN MY HASTE TO JOIN BATTLE, I MANAGED TO OFFEND THREE OTHERS.
BUMP
FIRST WAS HAMTHOS.
SWINE! I CHALLENGE YOU!
ACCEPTED!
AND THEN PORKIS!
K-THUMP
BRSSHH!
BUFFON! WE MUST DUEL!
BE WITH YOU IN A SECOND!
AND FINALLY ARAMPIGS.
TUMBLE!
BY MY SPATULA, WE DUEL!
TAKE A NUMBER!
CRASH

IT WAS THEN THAT A REALIZATION STRUCK ME. I HAD JUST CHALLENGED THREE DIFFERENT MINIONTEERS! COULD I DEFEAT THEM?
OOPSIES!
IT SEEMED UNLIKELY, FOR THEY WERE RUGGED INDIVIDUALS, AS NOBLE AS THE DAY IS LONG AND WELL-VERSED IN THE ART OF SPATULA-FIGHTING. STILL, AS A GASCON, I COULD ONLY DO AS MY FATHER HAD BADE ME.
WOOO WOOO! LET'S FIGHT!
DUELING, SIRS, IS ILLEGAL.
WHO DARES INTERRUPT?
A LOT OF US.
IT WAS CARDINAL CARDINALIEU'S GUARDS. EVIL MEN, ALL. THAT SAID, CREDIT MUST BE GIVEN WHERE CREDIT IS DUE, AND THE GUARD HAD CERTAINLY SPOKEN TRUTH: THERE WERE INDEED A LOT OF THEM.

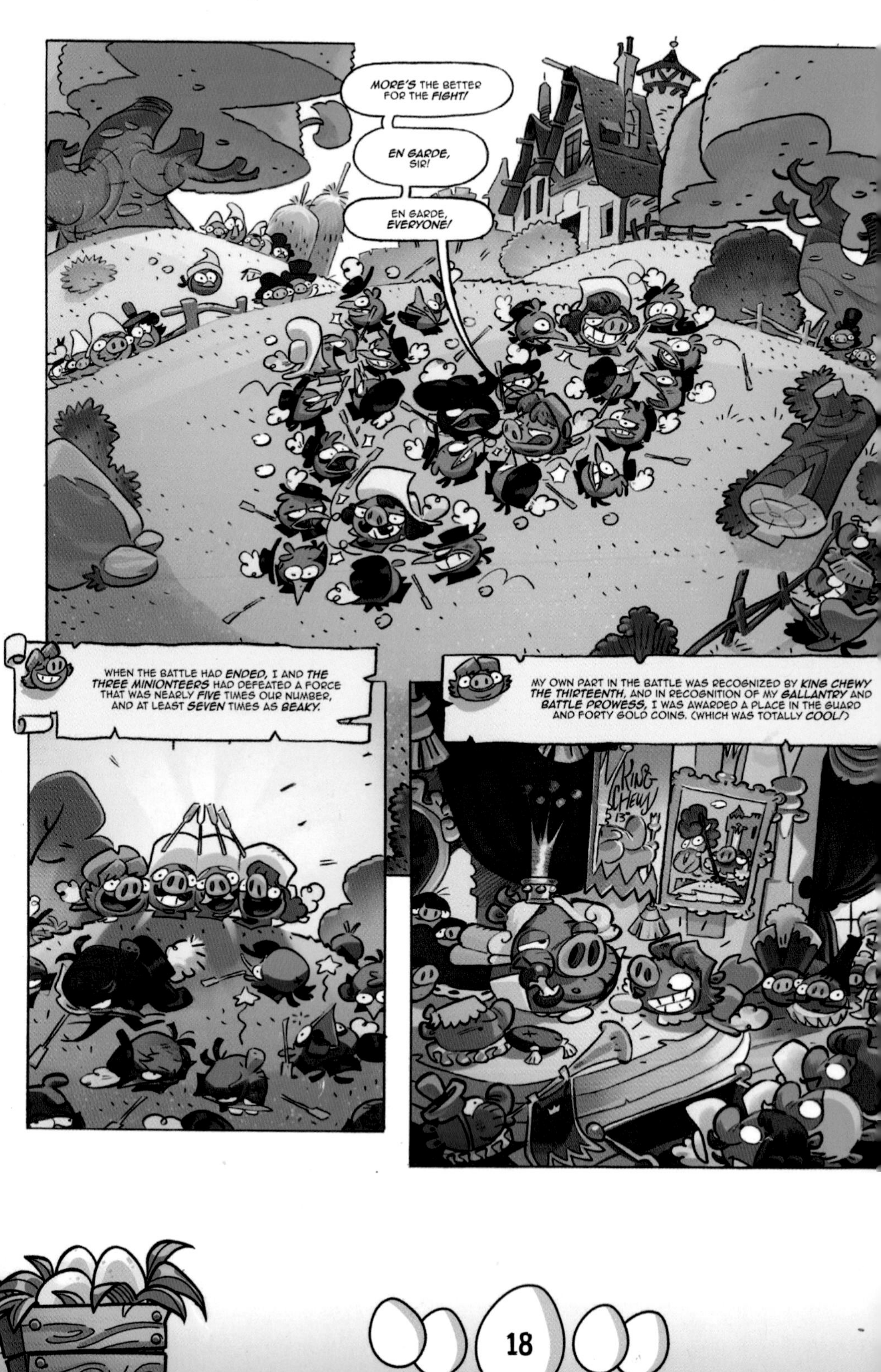
MORE'S THE BETTER FOR THE FIGHT!
EN GARDE, SIR!
EN GARDE, EVERYONE!
WHEN THE BATTLE HAD ENDED, I AND THE THREE MINIONTEERS HAD DEFEATED A FORCE THAT WAS NEARLY FIVE TIMES OUR NUMBER, AND AT LEAST SEVEN TIMES AS BEAKY.
MY OWN PART IN THE BATTLE WAS RECOGNIZED BY KING CHEWY THE THIRTEENTH, AND IN RECOGNITION OF MY GALLANTRY AND BATTLE PROWESS, I WAS AWARDED A PLACE IN THE GUARD AND FORTY GOLD COINS. (WHICH WAS TOTALLY COOL!)
KING CHEWY 13

IT WAS SHORTLY THEREAFTER THAT I FELL IN LOVE WITH A YOUNG WOMAN NAMED CONSTANCE. (ALSO TOTALLY COOL!)
MY BELOVED CONSTANCE WORKED WITH ANNE, THE QUEEN CONSORT OF FRANCE, A WOMAN WHO WAS HAVING A SECRET AFFAIR WITH THE DUKE OF BUCKINGHAM-N-EGGS.
HEY! ARE YOU TWO KISSING?
SHHHH! IT'S SECRET!
CONSTANCE BEGGED ME TO RETRIEVE JEWELS THAT ANNE HAD GIVEN TO THE DUKE, AS ANNE NEEDED TO WEAR THEM AT THE ROYAL HOG STOMP. IF THEY WERE NOT AROUND HER DELICATE NECK AT THE TIME OF THE DANCE, HER AFFAIR WOULD BE REVEALED!
I COULD NOT REFUSE MY LOVE CONSTANCE THIS REQUEST, FOR I WAS SO MUCH IN LOVE WITH HER THAT I COULD REFUSE HER NOTHING. NOTHING AT ALL!
PIZZA
COULD I HAVE THAT LAST SLICE OF PIZZA?
HUH? OH! UMM. UHH.... ERRRR...
QUITE UNFORTUNATELY, CARDINAL CARDINALIEU AND HIS EVIL GUARDS STOOD IN MY WAY!
EXCUSE ME, BUT COULD YOU STAND SOMEWHERE ELSE?

I COULD NOT HOPE TO WIN PAST THE BIRDS ALONE, BUT AS FATE WOULD HAVE IT, MY THREE NOBLE FRIENDS CAME TO THE RESCUE. HAMTHOS! PORKIS! AND ARAMPIGS!
ALL FOR ONE, AND ONE FOR ALL!
NOW, HOW SHALL WE HANDLE THIS?
YOU KNOW, PROPER DISCOURSE COULD LEAD TO AN EQUITABLE AGREEMENT. LET'S TALK TO THEM AND TRY TO WORK OUT A REASONABLE SOLUTION.
HA HA HA HA HA HA HA
HAW HAW HA HAW HAW HAW HA HAW
WE FIGHT!

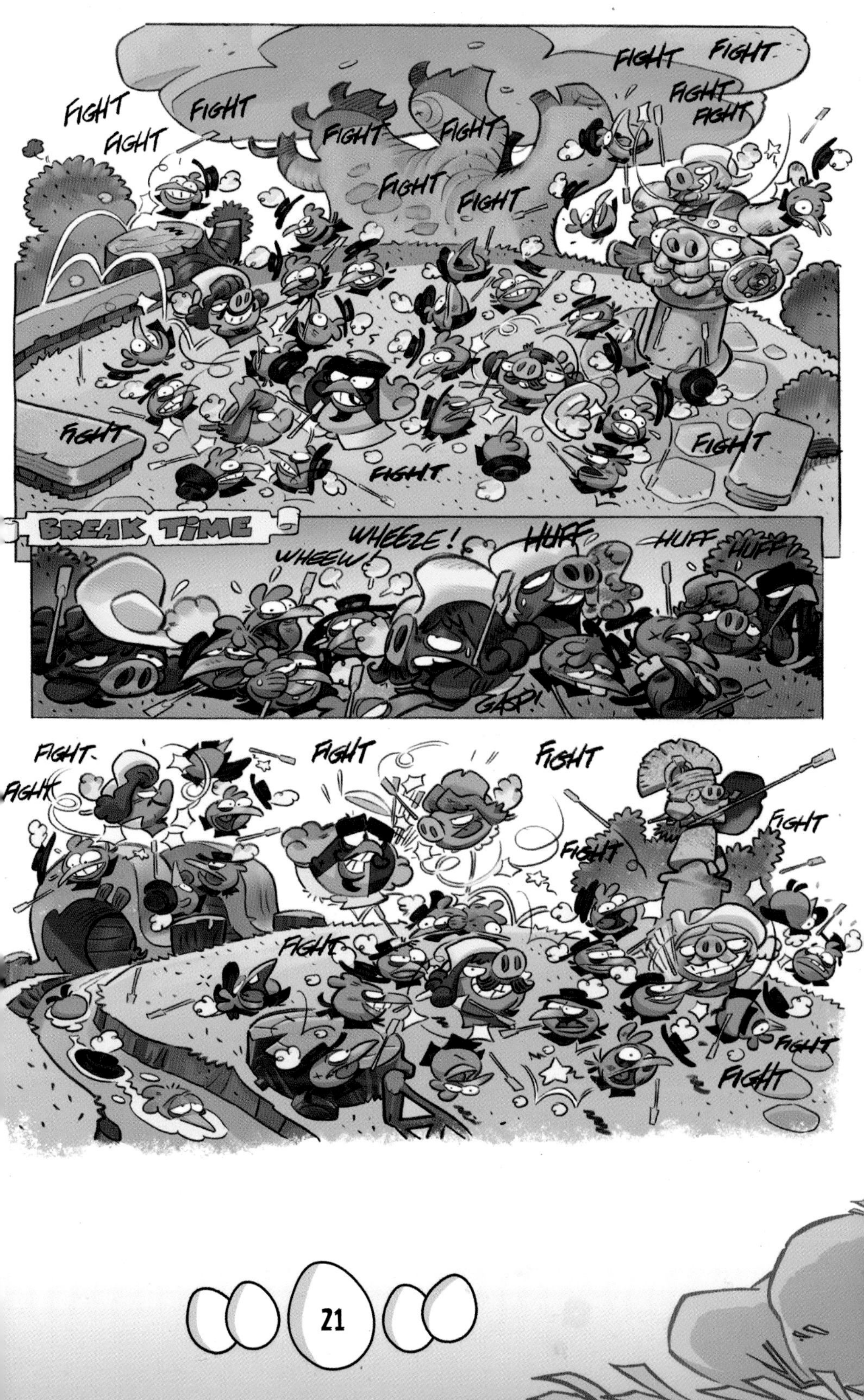
FIGHT
FIGHT
FIGHT
FIGHT
FIGHT
FIGHT
FIGHT
FIGHT
FIGHT
FIGHT
FIGHT
FIGHT
FIGHT
FIGHT
BREAK TIME
WHEEZE!
WHEEW!
HUFF
HUFF
HUFF
GASP!
FIGHT
FIGHT
FIGHT
FIGHT
FIGHT
FIGHT
FIGHT
FIGHT
FIGHT

VICTORY!
AND HERE'S THOSE JEWELS WE WERE LOOKING FOR!
ROYAL JEWELS! ALL FOR $1, AND $1 FOR ALL!
YOU GUYS ARE TOTALLY HEROES!
SMEK
SMEK
WE KNOW!
MUNCH
HA HA HA
HAH! LET'S EAT PIZZA!
MUNCH
MUNCH
HA HA
ANYBODY MIND IF I EAT THE LAST ONE?
WE FIGHT!
The end

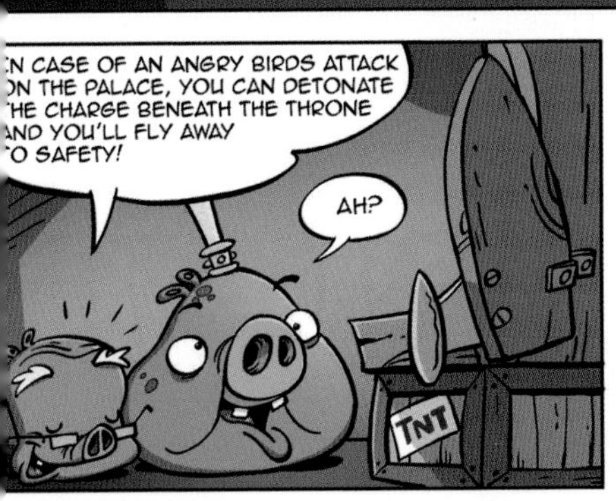

WRITTEN BY: PASCAL OOST • ART AND COLORS BY: THOMAS CABELLIC • LETTERS BY: ROVIO COMICS

ANGRY BIRDS™

THE JOKE

SPROING!

SOMETIMES, EVEN IN THE MIDST OF BATTLE, THERE IS A BIT OF TIME TO SPARE...

WANNA HEAR A JOKE?

AB 2014-011

THERE WERE THESE TWO PIGS AND THEIR BOSS, RIGHT? THEY WENT INTO A BAR...

WHISPER... TWO OYS- TERS... WHISPER... WHAT ARE PANTS?

WRITTEN BY: KARI KORHONEN • ART BY: CÉSAR FERIOLI • COLORS BY: DIGIKORE • LETTERS BY: PISARA OY

"TO THE RIGHT OF YOU!" HEH! HEH!
THAT'S PRETTY FUNNY!
AH! HAH! HAH! HAH! HOW STUPID CAN YOU GET!
HAH! HAH! PANTS! HAH! HAH! HAH! NYAH! AAH!
WHOOSH!
THUD!
?!
CAREFUL, FELLAS! THAT'S THE ONE THEY CALL "DA BOMB!"
WHY DIDN'T HE EXPLODE?
TEE! HEE! HEE! HEE! HEE!

MUAH! HAH! HAH! HAH! HAH! HAH!

"FACES LIKE MOTOR-MASCOTS!"

WELL THAT WAS CERTAINLY NEW.

SNORT! NYAH! HAH! HAH!

WHAT THE DEVIL WAS THAT?! NO BLAST?

I NEED TO GO AGAIN!

I CANNOT EXPLODE UNLESS I GET ***ANGRY!*** THINKING OF THAT JOKE TOOK ALL THE FIGHT OUT OF ME!

BUT THIS TIME I'LL ***CONCENTRATE!***

I WON'T... GIGGLE!... THINK ABOUT... THEIR SNOUTS!

WHUM!

MUAH HAH HAH HAH HAH!
YIKES!
SPLAT!
NYAH! HAH! HAH!
THIS IS TERRIBLE!
ME!
HAH! HAH!
THE MIGHTY WEAPON!
PARALYSED!
HAH! HAH!
WHAT IS HE LAUGHING AT?
AH! HAH! HAH!
"THREE TONS OF GORGONZOLA!"
WHAT'S SO DARN FUNNY ABOUT US?
HE SAID SOMETHING ABOUT OUR SNOUTS.
THE DAY CONTINUES IN VERY MUCH THE SAME VEIN...
AH! HAH! HAH!
PLEASE HELP!
MY TUMMY HURTS!

YOU, SIR, ARE HIDEOUS! SNORT! YAH! HAH! HAH!
IT GETS SO BAD THAT THE MERE SITE OF PIGS GETS BOMB GOING!
WAAAAH HAH HAH!
IF THIS KEEPS UP, WE'LL BE IN REAL TROUBLE! WHAT'S WRONG WITH HIM?
BEATS ME!
NYAH HAH HAH HAH HAH!
SPLAT!
IF IT ISN'T... HAH! HAH! ...THE PORCINE PRINCE! NYAH! AH!
THE BIG PIG! WEE! HEE! HEE! PREPOSTEROUS!
"YOUR FACE!" AH! HAH! HAH!
GUARDS!

WHAT? IS HE LAUGHING AT ME? IS THAT IT?
TEE HEE
HEE HEE
HEE
HEE
WHAT'S WRONG WITH ME? GIVE IT TO ME HONESTLY! WHAT'S SO FREAKING FUNNY?
WELL, YOU DO HAVE A GIANT SNOZZLE.
DONK!
YOU'RE ONE TO TALK! LOOK IN THE MIRROR LATELY?
OR DID THE MIRROR CRACK?
THIS RIDICULE IS UNLAWFUL! I DEMAND AN ENQUIRY!
HAH! HAH! HAH! HAH! HAH!
DARN!

HIS HOOTING IS TEARING US APART! SOON THERE'LL BE NOTHING TO LAUGH ABOUT!
THERE'S NOTHING HERE TO LAUGH ABOUT!
YOU ARE SUPPOSED TO GO BOOM! IT IS THE ONE THING ASKED OF YOU!
BUT IF A GIGGLING MORON IS WHAT YOU ARE NOW... I SUPPOSE WE'LL DO ALL THE WORK!
WHAT?!
I MAY BE A MORON...
...BUT I DO MY PART!
BOOM!

I GUESS YOU'VE STILL GOT IT!
THERE! WAS THAT SO HARD?
ARE YOU JUDGING ME TOO?
KA-BOOM!
SOON...
THE PIGS STOPPED THEIR ATTACK! LET'S SEE WHAT'S GOING ON!
SO, THE ROYAL FACE IS SOMETHING TO LAUGH ABOUT NOW, IS IT?

THE PIGS HAVE BECOME A SOURCE OF AMUSEMENT, EH? WE'LL SEE ABOUT THAT!

HOW'S THAT FOR A JOKE!

SOON BACK IN THE FORTRESS...

YOU WILL NOT HAVE THE LAST LAUGH! LET US GO!

TELL ME WHAT THE ROUND BLACK ONE WAS HOWLING ABOUT!

IF YOU DON'T, WE'VE GOT WAYS TO MAKE LITTLE BIRDIES ***SING!***

ELSEWHERE...

ALARM! THEY'VE GOT JAKE, JAY AND JIM!

YOU *DO NOT* DO THAT TO MY FRIENDS!
I WILL WIPE THAT GRIN OFF THEIR STUPID FACES OR MY NAME ISN'T...
STRETCH!
...DA BOMB!
AND SO...
YOU BOYS HAVE LEARNED YOUR LESSON, RIGHT?
THERE'S A TIME AND A PLACE FOR JOKES - EVEN GOOD ONES!
LET'S HEAR IT, THEN!
THERE WERE TWO PIGS...
I DON'T GET IT.
THE END

A MASTER PIG THEATER TALE

20,000 EGGS UNDER THE SEA

ANGRY BIRDS

IT WAS HARD TIMES IN LONDON THAT YEAR. SUPPLIES WERE LOW AND TEMPERS WERE HIGH. ESPECIALLY ON THE DOCKS.

NICE DAY, EH? YEAH?

YOU **THINK** SO? WANNA **FIGHT** ABOUT IT?

AB 2014-008

A MYSTERIOUS **SEA MONSTER** HAD BEEN DISRUPTING SHIPPING VESSELS, SENDING THEM TO THE BOTTOM OF THE OCEAN.

THIS MEANT THERE WAS LITTLE TRADE OF SUCH NECESSARY ITEMS AS **BUBBLEGUM, NESTING STRAW,** AND **BALLOONS.**

IT WAS THEN THAT I KNEW I MUST ASSEMBLE A TEAM OF **ADVENTURERS** WHO COULD PUT AN **END** TO THIS **MENACE.**

TERENCE. CHUCK. BOYS. GLAD YOU COULD MAKE IT.

YEAH. WELL, **BUBBLEGUM'S** GETTING LOW. GOTTA MAKE A **STAND** SOMETIME.

WRITTEN BY: PAUL TOBIN • ART BY: PACO RODRIQUES • COLORS BY: JOSEP DE HARO • LETTERS BY: PISARA OY

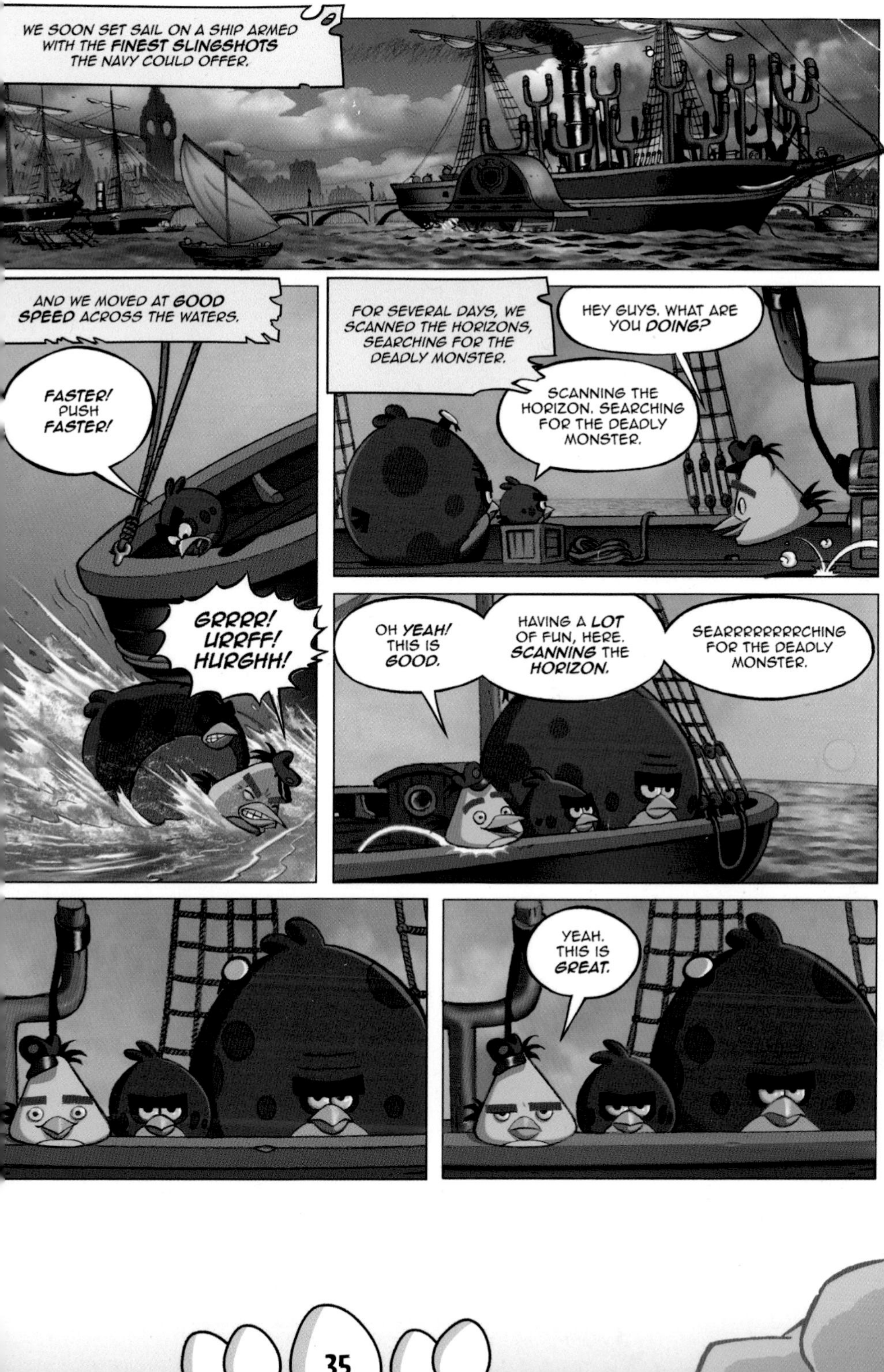

WE SOON SET SAIL ON A SHIP ARMED WITH THE **FINEST SLINGSHOTS** THE NAVY COULD OFFER.

AND WE MOVED AT **GOOD SPEED** ACROSS THE WATERS.

FASTER! PUSH **FASTER!**

GRRRR! URRFF! HURGHH!

FOR SEVERAL DAYS, WE SCANNED THE HORIZONS, SEARCHING FOR THE DEADLY MONSTER.

HEY GUYS. WHAT ARE YOU **DOING?**

SCANNING THE HORIZON. SEARCHING FOR THE DEADLY MONSTER.

OH YEAH! THIS IS GOOD.
HAVING A LOT OF FUN, HERE. SCANNING THE HORIZON.
SEARRRRRRRRCHING FOR THE DEADLY MONSTER.

YEAH. THIS IS GREAT.

AND THEN...

HEY. I THINK I SEE SOMETHING.

WE LAUNCHED THE **FIERCEST BARRAGE** IN THE **HISTORY** OF WARFARE.

HELLO.

HUNDREDS OF CANNONBALLS MADE THEIR WAY THROUGH THE AIR LIKE A **SWARM OF ANGRY CROWS**, IF CROWS WERE **ROUND** AND MADE OF **METAL.**

IT PROVED INEFFECTUAL.

UH-OH. ANYONE HAVE A **BACKUP PLAN?**

DINK

K-DINK

MY BACKUP PLAN IS TO BACK UP!
BACK UP! BACK UP!

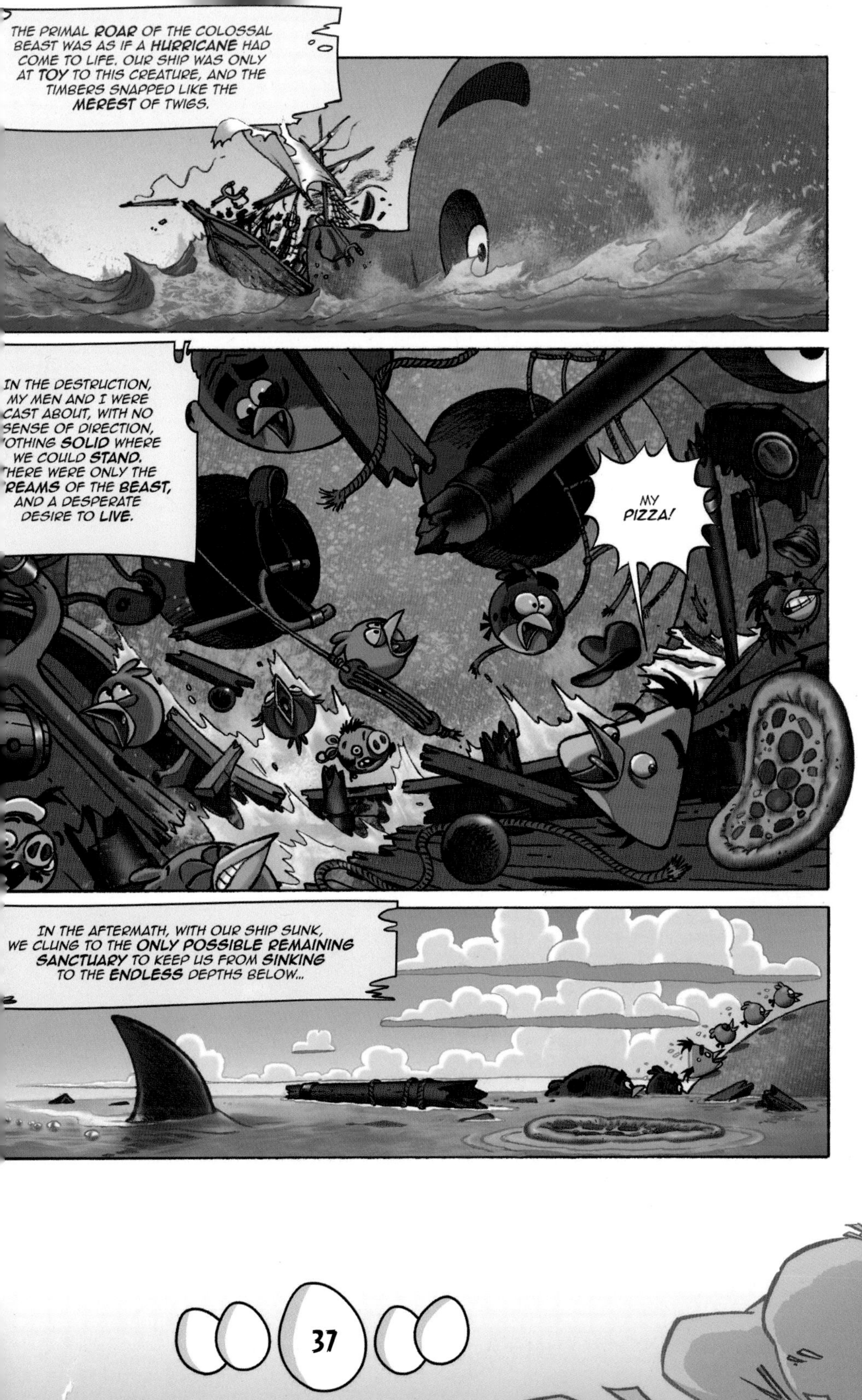
THE PRIMAL ROAR OF THE COLOSSAL BEAST WAS AS IF A HURRICANE HAD COME TO LIFE. OUR SHIP WAS ONLY AT TOY TO THIS CREATURE, AND THE TIMBERS SNAPPED LIKE THE MEREST OF TWIGS.
IN THE DESTRUCTION, MY MEN AND I WERE CAST ABOUT, WITH NO SENSE OF DIRECTION, OTHING SOLID WHERE WE COULD STAND. HERE WERE ONLY THE REAMS OF THE BEAST, AND A DESPERATE DESIRE TO LIVE.
MY PIZZA!
IN THE AFTERMATH, WITH OUR SHIP SUNK, WE CLUNG TO THE ONLY POSSIBLE REMAINING SANCTUARY TO KEEP US FROM SINKING TO THE ENDLESS DEPTHS BELOW...

THE CREATURE ITSELF.

HEY... THIS ISN'T FLESH. IT'S... METAL.
TONK! TONK! TONK!

OF COURSE IT'S METAL. IT'S A SUBMARINE.

COME BELOW AND I'LL TELL THE TALE, BIRDLINGS.

IT SEEMED WE WERE THE GUESTS OF AN OUTRAGEOUS CREATURE, CAPTAIN PIGO, THE CAPTAIN OF THE PIGGILUS.

A VAST SUBMARINE, SHAPED AS A SWINE.
PIGO HIMSELF PROVED TO BE A GRUMPY BUT CULTURED OUTCAST, AND THE SUBMARINE WAS FULL OF WONDERS MOST STRANGE.
YOU BIRDS MUST BE HUNGRY. HERE'S A BUFFET. AND ALSO A DISCO.
PIGO HAD REMOVED HIMSELF FROM SOCIETY AND THE IGNORANCE OF THE MASSES, WHO COULD NOT UNDERSTAND HIS SCIENTIFIC GENIUS.
A HOVERING TOASTER, GENTLEMAN. A HOVERING TOASTER.
OOOO.
NOW, HE SAILED BENEATH THE SEAS ON A QUEST FOR SCIENTIFIC KNOWLEDGE, SEARCHING OUT WONDERS NEVER BEFORE SEEN BY MAN.
STOP
BUT THERE WAS A GREATER QUEST. ONE THAT HAD ELUDED PIGO FOR ALL HIS YEARS.
EGGS, MEN. I SEARCH FOR EGGS. BUT NOT JUST ANY EGGS! I SEARCH FOR THE LEGENDARY OCTO-BIRD'S EGGS!
TAP TAP
TAP

DESPITE THE DESTRUCTION OF OUR SHIP, AND WHAT AMOUNTED TO OUR KIDNAPPING, WE BEGAN TO BE FRIENDS WITH THE RECLUSIVE CAPTAIN PIGO, SPENDING MANY DAYS IN QUIET REVERIE AND CONTEMPLATION.
HAH! TAKE THAT!
FINISH HIM!
AND WITNESSING THE STRANGEST OF WONDERS WHILE TWENTY THOUSAND LEAGUES BENEATH THE SEA.
I RECALL SUCH WONDERS AS THE ELECTRIC EEL, WHICH MADE THE OCEAN DEPTHS AS BRIGHT AS ANY LONDON STREET.
TURN THAT OFF! I'M TRYING TO SLEEP!
AND A THEME PARK WITH THE LARGEST WATER SLIDE I'D EVER SEEN.
19,998 LEAGUES
19,999 LEAGUES
20,000 LEAGUES
AND THEN CAME THE DAY WHEN THE ALARM BELLS RANG.
DING DING DING
SHOOP

HE OCTO-BIRD HAD BEEN SIGHTED.
MAN THE TORPEDOES!
HARD TO STARBOARD!
SEAL ALL HATCHES!
ALL STATIONS PREPARE FOR BATTLE, AND, MEN...
YES SIR?
RECORD MY FAVORITE CARTOONS. I DON'T WANT TO MISS THEM.
SECONDS LATER, THE BATTLE BEGAN. THE LASHING TENTACLES OF THE GREAT OCTO-BIRD STRUCK THE WALLS OF OUR SUBMARINE. THERE WAS A NOISE LIKE A HUNDRED THOUSAND BURSTS OF THUNDER.

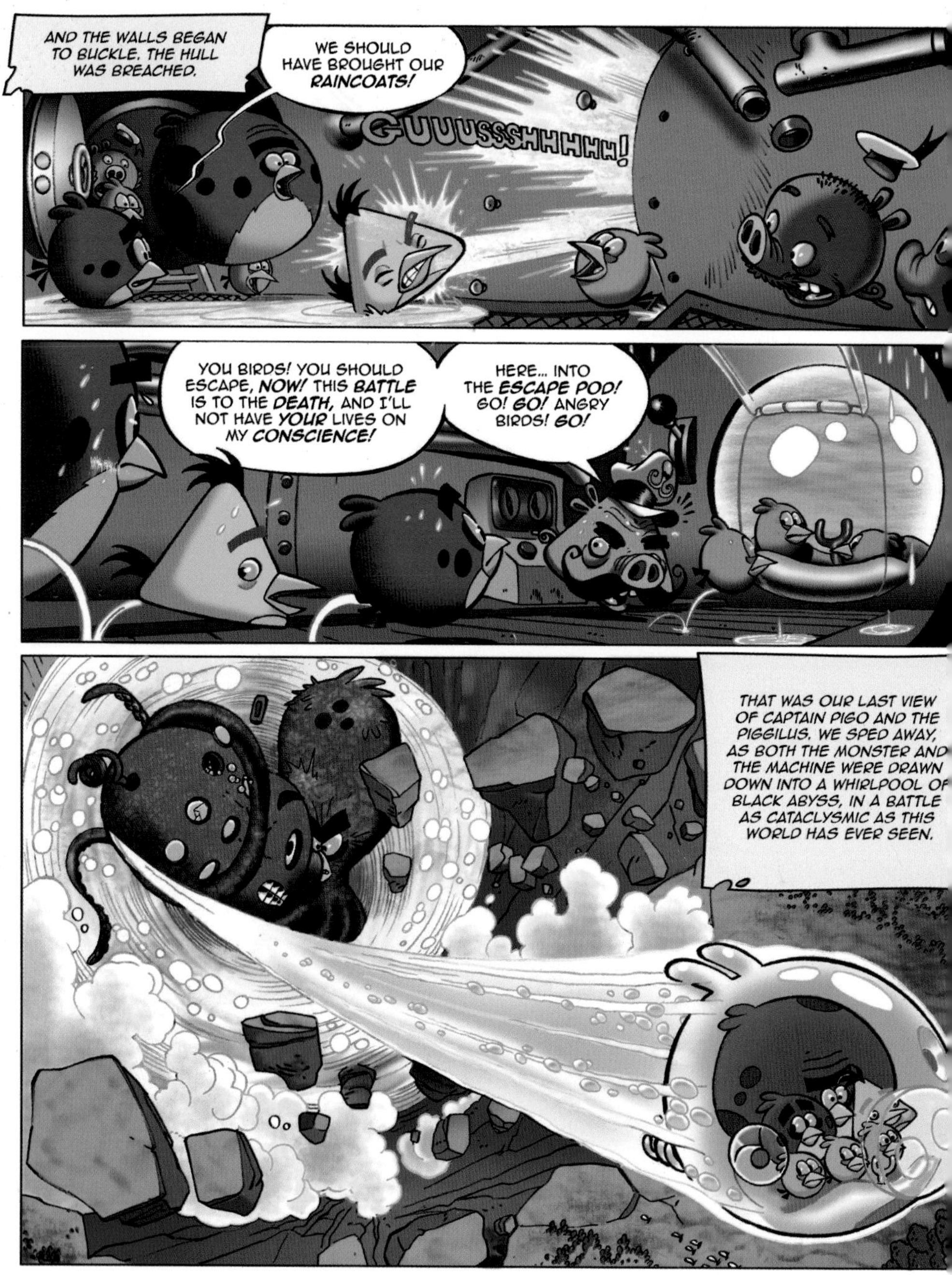

AND THE WALLS BEGAN TO BUCKLE. THE HULL WAS BREACHED.

WE SHOULD HAVE BROUGHT OUR *RAINCOATS!*

GUUUSSSHHHHH!

YOU BIRDS! YOU SHOULD ESCAPE, *NOW!* THIS *BATTLE* IS TO THE *DEATH,* AND I'LL NOT HAVE *YOUR* LIVES ON MY *CONSCIENCE!*

HERE... INTO THE *ESCAPE POD!* GO! *GO!* ANGRY BIRDS! *GO!*

THAT WAS OUR LAST VIEW OF CAPTAIN PIGO AND THE PIGGILUS. WE SPED AWAY, AS BOTH THE MONSTER AND THE MACHINE WERE DRAWN DOWN INTO A WHIRLPOOL OF BLACK ABYSS, IN A BATTLE AS CATACLYSMIC AS THIS WORLD HAS EVER SEEN.

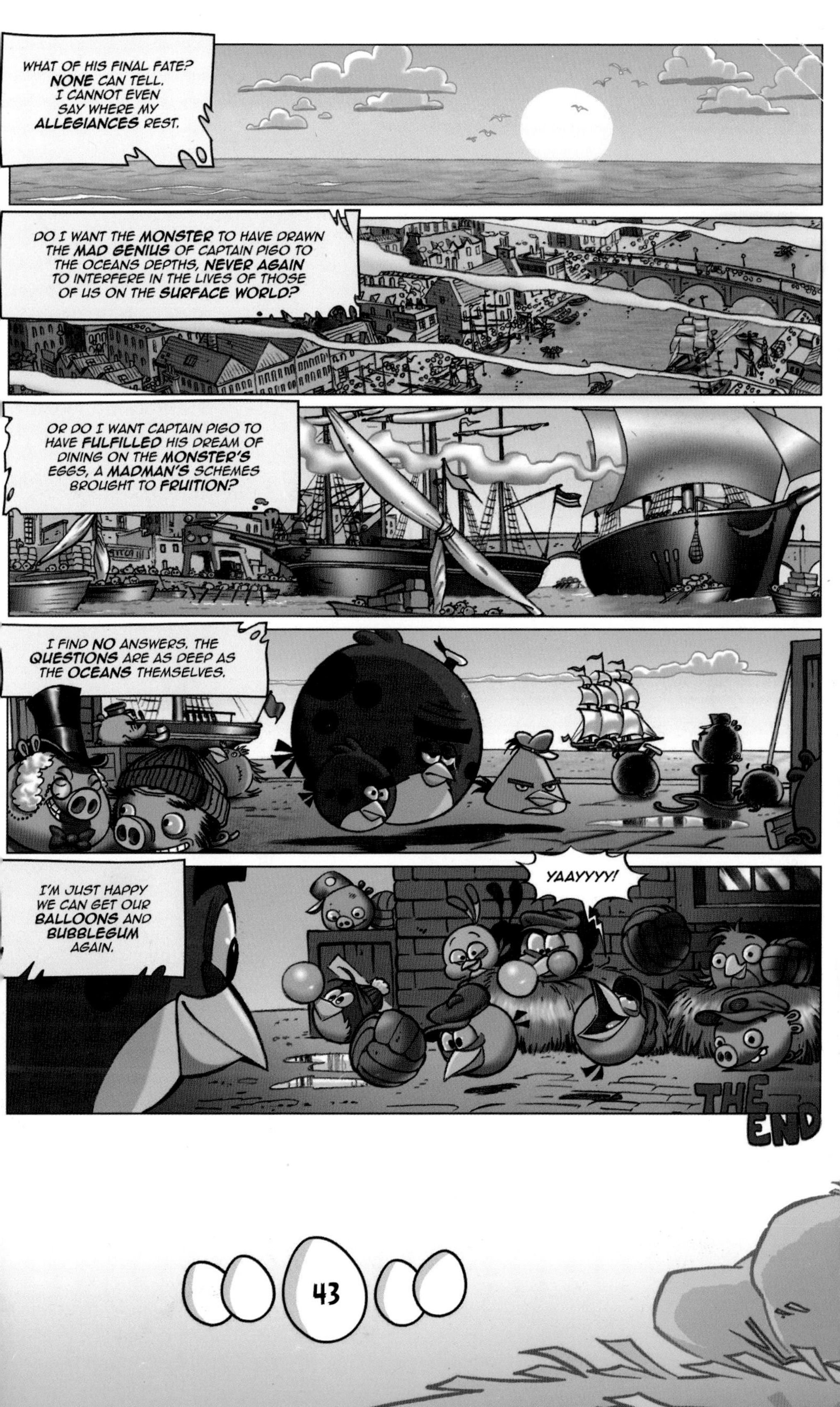
WHAT OF HIS FINAL FATE? NONE CAN TELL. I CANNOT EVEN SAY WHERE MY ALLEGIANCES REST.
DO I WANT THE MONSTER TO HAVE DRAWN THE MAD GENIUS OF CAPTAIN PIGO TO THE OCEANS DEPTHS, NEVER AGAIN TO INTERFERE IN THE LIVES OF THOSE OF US ON THE SURFACE WORLD?
OR DO I WANT CAPTAIN PIGO TO HAVE FULFILLED HIS DREAM OF DINING ON THE MONSTER'S EGGS, A MADMAN'S SCHEMES BROUGHT TO FRUITION?
I FIND NO ANSWERS. THE QUESTIONS ARE AS DEEP AS THE OCEANS THEMSELVES.
I'M JUST HAPPY WE CAN GET OUR BALLOONS AND BUBBLEGUM AGAIN.
YAAYYYY!
THE END

BAD PIGGIES
EJECTOR THRONE 2
I APOLOGIZE FOR ANY INCONVENIENCE CAUSED BY MY EJECTOR THRONE! BUT I ASSURE YOU: THAT WON'T HAPPEN FOR A SECOND TIME!
MMMPH...
TNT
AB 2013-07

SEE? THE PALACE NOW CONTAINS DESIGNATED EXITS TO ENSURE SAFE AND PAINLESS PASSAGE IN CASE OF ANGRY BIRDS ATTACKS!
HI!

IF YOU WOULD BE SO KIND TO PRESS THE BUTTON FOR THIS SECOND TEST.
MAYBE I COULD TRY...

BANG!

PERFECT!
THIS TIME THE THRONE AND ITS OCCUPIER ARE TRANSPORTED SAFELY AWAY FRO ANY POSSIBLE HARM!

NOW FOR THE NEXT PHASE, I MUST ENVISION A MEANS FOR A SOFT LANDING...
AAAAAHHH...

THE END

WRITTEN BY: PASCAL OOST • ART AND COLORS BY: THOMAS CABELLIC • LETTERS BY: ROVIO COMICS

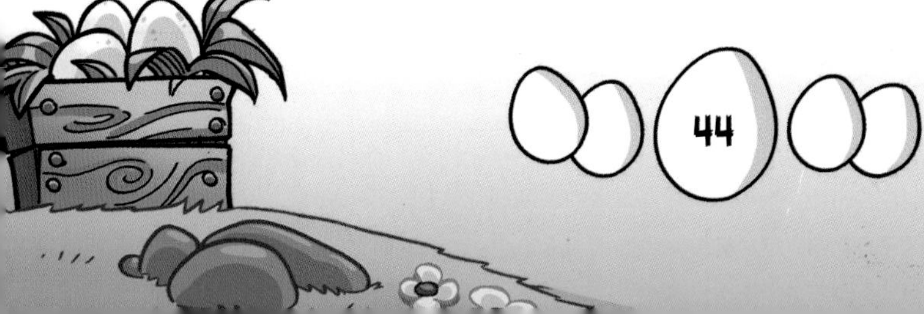

WRITTEN BY: JANNE TORISEVA • ART BY: CÉSAR FERIOLI • COLORS BY: DIGIKORE • LETTERS BY: PISARA OY

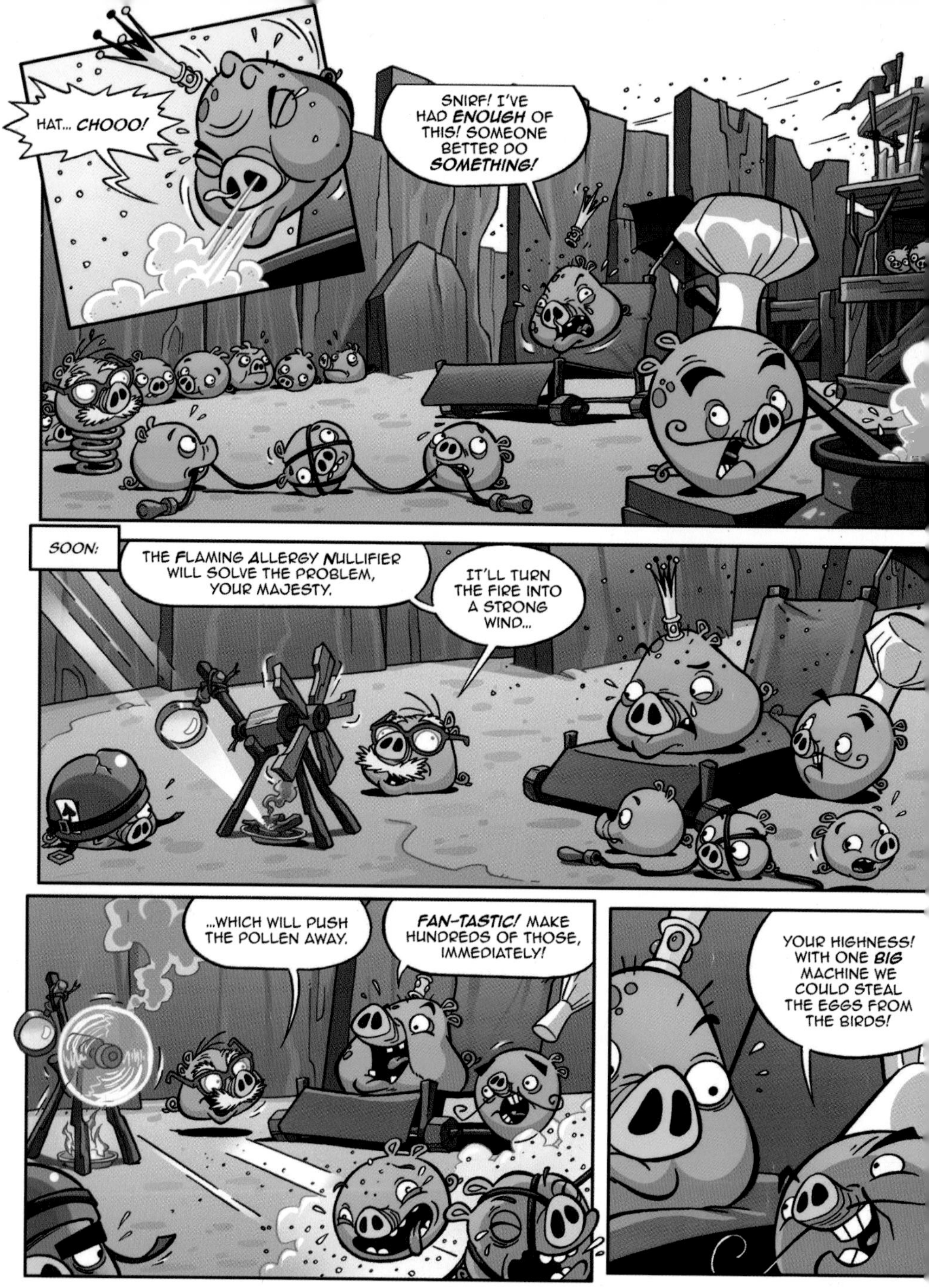

HAT... *CHOOO!*

SNIRF! I'VE HAD **ENOUGH** OF THIS! SOMEONE BETTER DO ***SOMETHING!***

SOON:

THE **F**LAMING **A**LLERGY **N**ULLIFIER WILL SOLVE THE PROBLEM, YOUR MAJESTY.

IT'LL TURN THE FIRE INTO A STRONG WIND...

HMM... THE WIND IS RISING.
YOU-HEAVE-HO!
?
WHAT ARE YOU LARDBALLS DOING HERE?
TURN THE GLASS!
YES, BOSS!
HEY! -SNIFF- TURN THAT THING OFF!
HATCHOOO!
GO GET THE EGGS!
YES, BOSS!

LOOK AT THOSE CLOUDS, GUYS!
LET'S GET BACK TO OUR MATES.
AYE.

WHAT'S WRONG WITH RED?
AND WHERE ARE THE EGGS?
AND WHAT IS THAT?
-SNEEZE- THE PIGS
HATCHOO!

PIGS!
LET'S HOPE THAT THEY ARE NOT TOO FAR ALREADY!

BLUE BIRDS APPROACHING!

PUSH FASTER, YOU LAZY PORK!

I'M DOING MY BEST!

THERE ARE MORE OF THOSE MACHINES. WHAT ARE THEY?

DUNNO, BUT I DON'T LIKE 'EM. THEY'RE TOO WINDY.

WINDY...? GUYS, WE MIGHT STILL HAVE A CHANCE!

MY DEAR EGGS! WELCOME HOME!

CHEF, WHAT ARE YOU WAITING FOR? MAKE ME AN OMELETTE!
WHAT'S THAT HUMMING SOUND BEHIND THE GATE...

IT WORKS!

OH NO, THE EGG-WAGON!
IT'LL CRASH INTO THE WALL!
HURRY, LET'S TURN THESE MACHINES OFF!
JUST IN TIME!

LET'S GET THE EGGS BEFORE THE PIGS WAKE UP!

OUCH... WHAT HAPPENED?
OH NO, WE'LL NEVER GET AWAY IN TIME!

WAIT... I THINK I GOT AN IDEA!

MY EGGS, WHERE ARE THEY?
LOOK, YOUR MAJESTY!

WHAT ARE YOU WAITING FOR? DO SOMETHING!
WE CAN'T CATCH 'EM. THEY'RE TOO FAST.

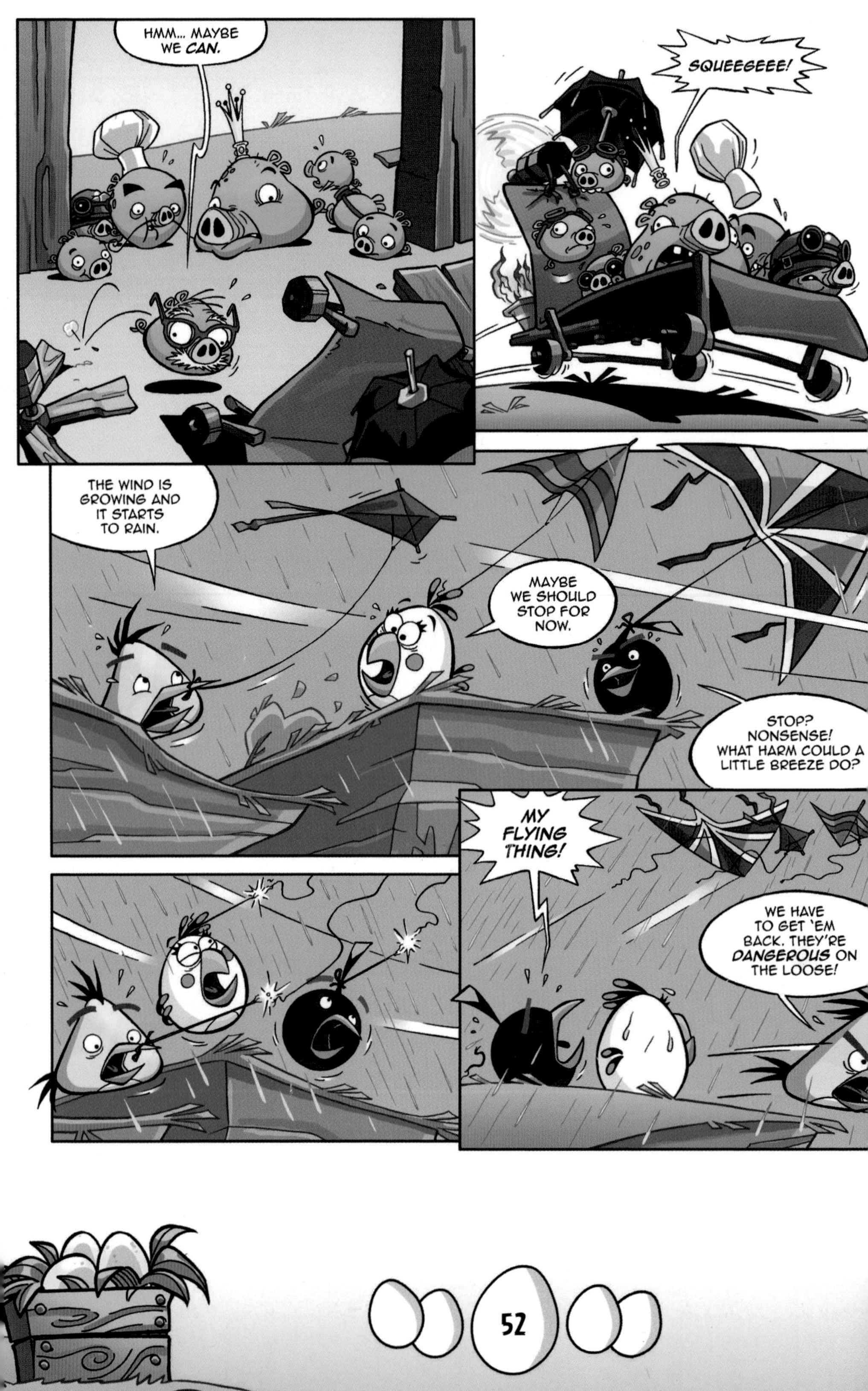
HMM... MAYBE WE CAN.
SQUEEEGEEE!
THE WIND IS GROWING AND IT STARTS TO RAIN.
MAYBE WE SHOULD STOP FOR NOW.
STOP? NONSENSE! WHAT HARM COULD A LITTLE BREEZE DO?
MY FLYING THING!
WE HAVE TO GET 'EM BACK. THEY'RE DANGEROUS ON THE LOOSE!

THE PIGS ARE COPYING US! HOW RUDE!
DON'T WORRY, THEY CAN'T CATCH US. THEIR LOAD IS TOO HEAVY.

WHY ARE WE SLOWING DOWN?

OH NO, THE RAIN EXTINGUISHED THE FIRE!

CHEF, GET READY TO BOIL SOME EGGS!
YES, YOUR HIGHNESS!

HUH?

SQUEAL!

PHEW! THAT WAS AT THE LAST MOMENT!

BUT WHAT IN THE WORLD ARE *THOSE?*

EGGS!

PIGS!

OUR FLYING THINGS

MAYBE IT'S BETTER THIS WAY, BOMB.

BUT WHAT SHALL WE DO WITH THESE BACON BADDIES?

HMM... I SAY LET'S SEND THEM...

...WHERE THE WIND BLOWS!

THE EN

ANGRY BIRDS™
GONE TO SEED
AB 2014-002

OUR STORY BEGINS IN THE REDWOOD FOREST...
KRAKKKA-BAA-ROOOOOM
HA HA HA HA HA HA HA!

DID YOU KIDS STARTLE BOMB INTO EXPLODING AGAIN?
NO!
UMMM, MAYBE.
HA HA HA HA HA!

YOU KNOW, MAYBE IT'S TIME TO DO SOMETHING MORE CONSTRUCTIVE WITH YOUR TIME.
HOW ABOUT SPYING ON THE PIGS?
OR HELPING FIGHT THE PIGS?
ISN'T THERE SOMETHING WE CAN STEAL FROM THEM?
NO, NO, DON'T YOU START WITH THAT.

HOW ABOUT GARDENING?
HELLO!
WH... WHAT?
OH NO.
GASP!

WRITTEN BY: JANNE TORISEVA • ART BY: MARCO GERVASIO • COLORS BY: DIGIKORE • LETTERS BY: PISARA OY

AN HOUR LATER.
SEE, YOU JUST PREPARE THE GROUND BY **HOEING** AND **RAKING.**
RAKE
RAKE
RAKE
GRUMBLE
GRUMBLE
GRUMBLE
SCRATCH SCRATCH

A DAY LATER.
AND WE DROP THE **SEEDS** IN OUR ROWS.
GRUMBLE GRUMBLE
GRUMBLE

A DAY LATER.
I HAVE THIS **SPECIAL PLANT FOOD** I MAKE FROM MUD FROM THE GEYSERS. IT'S **VERY** RICH IN **NUTRIENTS.**
HMMPF!
HMMPF!
HMMPF!

A WEEK LATER.
SEE? THE PLANTS GROW **EXTRAORDINARILY** FAST.
HEY, THIS IS KIND OF... **FUN!**

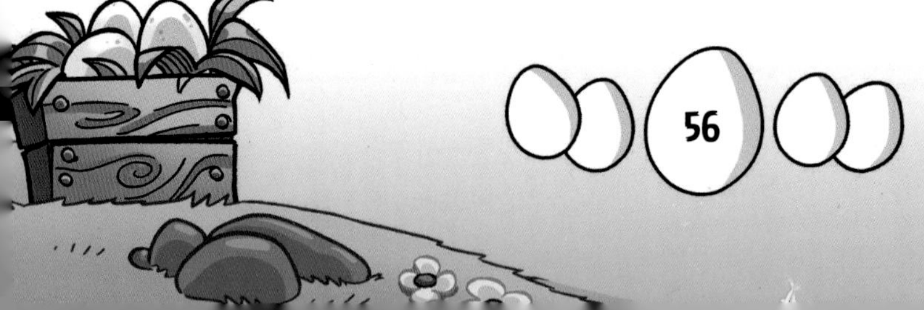

WATERMELON, CUCUMBERS, RHUBARB, SUGAR CANE, POTATOES!
EVERYTHING'S GROWING!

AND HERE, TASTE THESE STRAWBERRIES FRESH FROM OUR GARDEN!
MUNCH
SLURP
WOW! THESE ARE DELICIOUS!
MUNCH

SO ARE THESE GRAPES! DELICIOUS!
AND THE CANTALOUPES! DELICIOUS!
YOU KNOW WHAT'S REALLY DELICIOUS? THESE PEAS!

DELICIOUS!
DELICIOUS!
SOOOOO DELICIOUS!

ARE THEY TALKING ABOUT EGGS?
NO. SOMETHING ELSE.
SHOULD WE, I MEAN, YOU THINK, MAYBE WE COULD... UMM...

IF YOU WERE GOING TO SUGGEST WE STEAL EVERYTHING, AND EAT IT, AND ALSO STEAL THE SEEDS AND MAKE OUR OWN GARDEN, AND EAT THAT, THEN...

YESSSSSS!!!

THE NEXT DAY...
WELL, THE THREE OF YOU ARE CERTAINLY UP EARLY.
YEP!
IT'S BECAUSE WE LOVE GARDENING!
WE DO! I WONDER IF ANYTHING NEW SPROUTED TODAY! MAYBE THERE'LL BE SOME...

UHHH.
GAHHH!
OH NO.

AHHHHHHHHHH!

MEANWHILE... IN PIGGY CASTLE.
GOBBLE GOBBLE
SLOBBER GOBBLE
AND THE BIRDS GREW ALL OF THIS?

SLOBBER SLOBBER
THEY DID! WE WATCHED THEM!
WE THINK WE KNOW HOW TO DO IT!

AND THESE THINGS ARE TASTY, YOUR HIGHNESS?
THEY'RE NOT NEARLY AS GOOD AS EGGS.
NOTHING IS AS GOOD AS EGGS.
BUT THESE ARE... EDIBLE.

SNORK SLOBBER
GOBBLE GOBBLE GOBBLE

PERHAPS YOU SHOULD GROW SOME MORE.

AND SO...

RAKE

RAKE

THEY WERE USING RAKES AND HOES, LIKE THIS.

SCRATCH

SCRATCH

STAB

STAB

AND THEN THEY MADE *HOLES* IN THE *DIRT!*

AFTER *THAT,* THEY PUT *SEEDS* INSIDE THE *HOLES.*

SHOVEL

SHOVEL

SHOVEL

POUR THEM *ALL* IN.

SHAKE

SHAKE

SHAKE

YEAH! WHY WASTE TIME?

GOOD IDEA.

AND THEN THEY USED THIS *MUD* FROM THE GEYSERS. I GUESS IT MAKES THE PLANTS *GROW FASTER.*

HOW MUCH MUD DID THEY *USE?*

WHAT'S IT *MATTER?* USE IT *ALL.*

KERR-

FLOPP!!!...

AND **NOW** WHAT?

WE **WAIT,** I GUESS.

YOU MEAN, DO **NOTHING?** I'M **REALLY** GOOD AT THAT.

SPROUD

EHHH?

ALREADY STARTING TO **GROW?**

SPROUD

THAT'S **GREAT!**

POIK

BOIK

I SUPPOSE. BUT I WAS LOOKING **FORWARD** TO DOING A LOT OF **NOTHING.**

POIK

SPROUD

POIK

SKRUNK

!

GROW

GROW

GROW

SKRUNK

UHHHHHHH OH.

ARE THEY GOING TO *STOP?*
IT DOESN'T *LOOK* LIKE IT. MAYBE WE SHOULD *DO SOMETHING?*
AGAIN, I *WAS* LOOKING FORWARD TO DOING *NOTHING.*

OOOO! I'VE GOT AN *IDEA* OF WHAT WE COULD *DO!*
WHAT'S THAT?

RUNNNNNNN!!!

THE PLANTS ARE *CATCHING US!!!*
RUUUMBLE

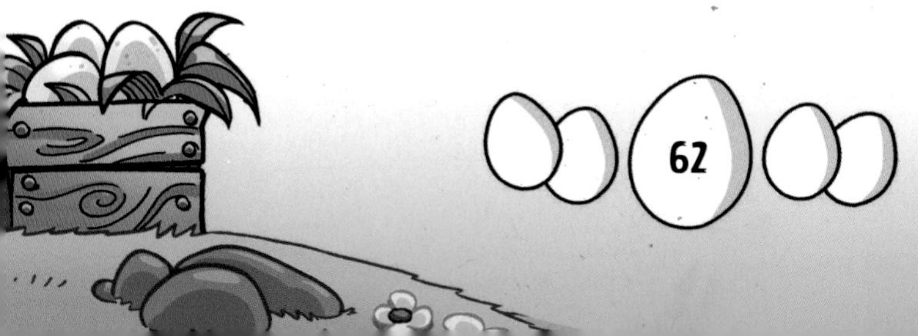

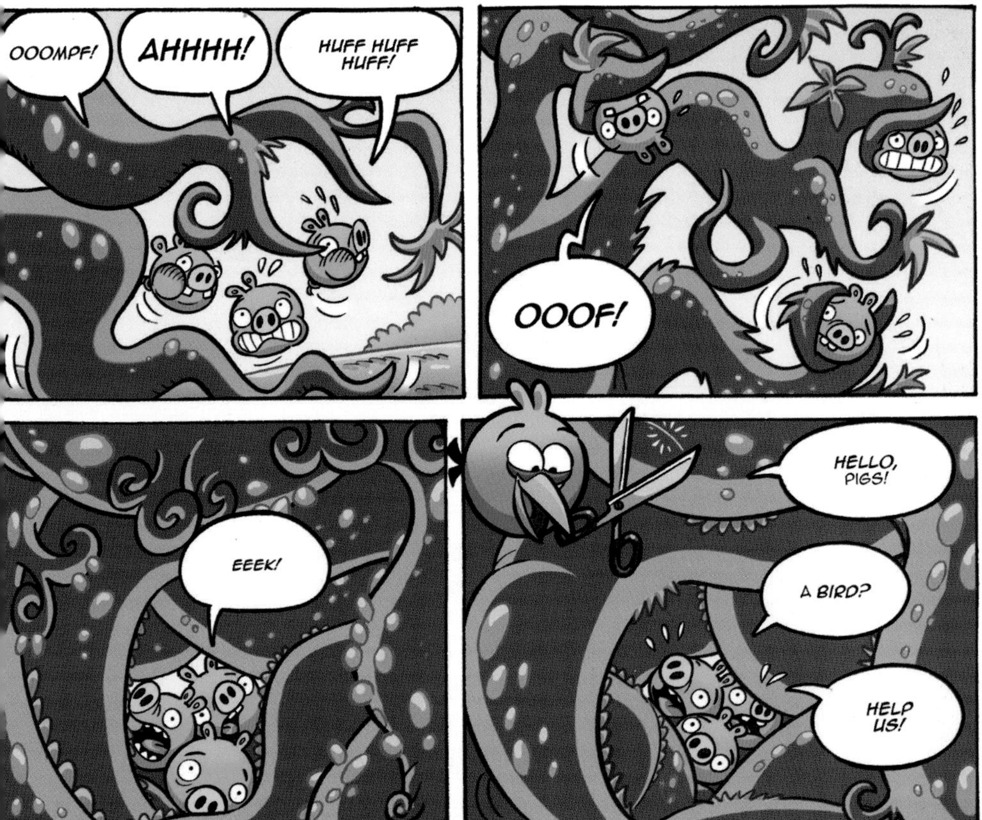

OOOMPF!
AHHHH!
HUFF HUFF HUFF!
OOOF!
EEEK!
HELLO, PIGS!
A BIRD?
HELP US!
WELL, WE *DO* KNOW THE WAY OUT, BUT... ***WHY*** SHOULD WE HELP ***YOU?***
YEAH. YOU'RE ***PIGS.***
AND WE'RE ***BIRDS.***
PLEASE, WE'LL DO ***ANYTHING!***
ANYTHING?
YES!

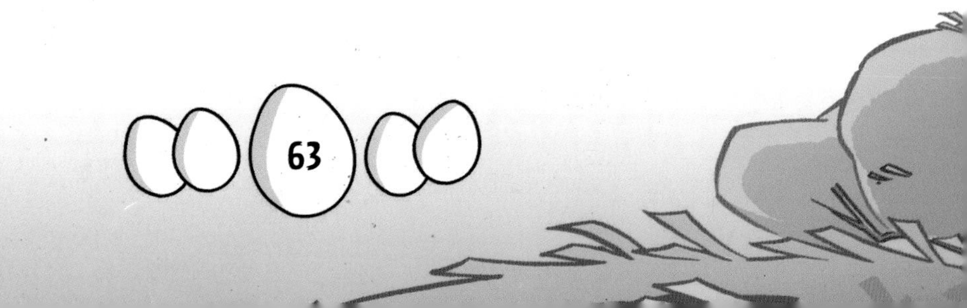

THE NEXT DAY.

HMMM. YOU KIDS ARE HAVING A DAY AT THE BEACH? I THOUGHT YOU'D BE WORKING ON YOUR GARDEN. DON'T YOU ENJOY THE STRAWBERRIES? THE WATERMELON?
WELL, SURE.
BUT IT'S A LOT OF WORK.
SO WE BROUGHT IN SOME HELPERS.

HUFF HUFF HUFF!
GUHH! GAHHH!
THE END

NGRY BIRDS™

THE CARECROW

AB 2013-024

ONE DAY, IN THE ROYAL GARDENS...

ERR, CORPORAL PIG – WHY HAS IT GONE *DARK?*

MY NEW *CREATION,* YOUR MAJESTY!

A SCARECROW! ACCORDING TO OLD TALES, IT'S THE ONE TRUE WAY TO SCARE BIRDS!

WELL IT CERTAINLY SCARES ME! I HOPE IT ISN'T CRUSHING MY NEW GARDEN GNOMES!

WE'LL FRIGHTEN THOSE ANGRY BIRDS AND SNATCH THEIR *EGGS!* THOSE FEATHERED FOOLS DON'T STAND A CHANCE THIS TIME!

WRITTEN BY: **GLENN DAKIN** • ART BY: **CÉSAR FERIOLI** • COLORS BY: **DIGIKORE** • LETTERS BY: **PISARA OY**

DAWN BREAKS OVER THE COBALT PLATEAU...
TO REVEAL...
YIKES! WHERE DID THAT COME FROM? WHA - WHAT IS IT?
IT - IT'S MAKING ME SHIV-ER AND SHAKE! BUT I DON'T KNOW WHY!
IT'S A SCARECROW! THE TRADITIONAL ENEMY OF THE BIRD RACE!
SUDDENLY...
IT - IT'S MOVING!
LOOK OUT!
BOMB'S EXPLODED WITH FRIGHT!
KA-BOOM!

IT'S TAKING THE **NEST!** STOP IT!

I CAN'T! IT - IT'S TOO BIG AND S-SCARY!

LOOK! IT'S CRUSHING EVERYTHING IN ITS PATH!

WHERE ARE THE BLUES? THEY'RE PLAYING OUT HERE SOMEWHERE! I HOPE THEY DON'T GET **STOMPED!**

AND WHERE **ARE** THE BLUES?

THREE THOUSAND AND ONE, THREE THOUSAND AND TWO -- RED WAS RIGHT, SKIPPING IS GOOD EXERCISE!

WHO'S TRYING TO DISTURB OUR EXERCISE?

OOPS!

TIMBERRR!

I TOLD YOU SKIPPING WAS USEFUL!

KRUMMP!

RED -- DID YOU SAVE THE **NEST?**

YOU - YOU **COULD** SAY THAT!

IT - IT'S JUST A GIANT **PUPPET** - WITH **PIGS** IN IT!

DON'T **HURT** US! IT WASN'T OUR IDEA! WE - WE DIDN'T WANT TO BE A SCARECROW!

A SCARECROW? **WE** AREN'T **CROWS** YOU **DOOFUS!**

NOW THIS BROKEN HEAD REALLY DOES LOOK SCARY...

HMM... LET'S TEACH THOSE PIGS A **LESSON...!**

THAT NIGHT, AT THE PIG PALACE...
A LOVELY NIGHT FOR A STROLL ALONG THE BATTLEMENTS! I WONDER IF I'LL BE GETTING AN EGG SUPPER TONIGHT?
I'M SURE YOU WILL, YOUR MAJESTY!
SUDDENLY...
WOOOH! I AM THE ZOMBIE OF THE COBALT PLATEAU! I SMELL JUICY PIG FLESH! YUM!
HELLLP! ZOMBIE ATTACK!
RUN!
SAVE YOUR BACON!
EEK! OWCH!
AND...
NOW YOU KNOW WHAT IT'S LIKE BEING SCARED! YOU CAN HAVE YOUR SILLY TOY BACK NOW!
AND...
WELL AT LEAST IT HAS ONE MORE USE...
...GIVING YOU THE BOOT! UNTIL YOU CAN COME UP WITH SOMETHING BETTER!
OW! YES, YOUR HIGHNESS! EEK!
THE END

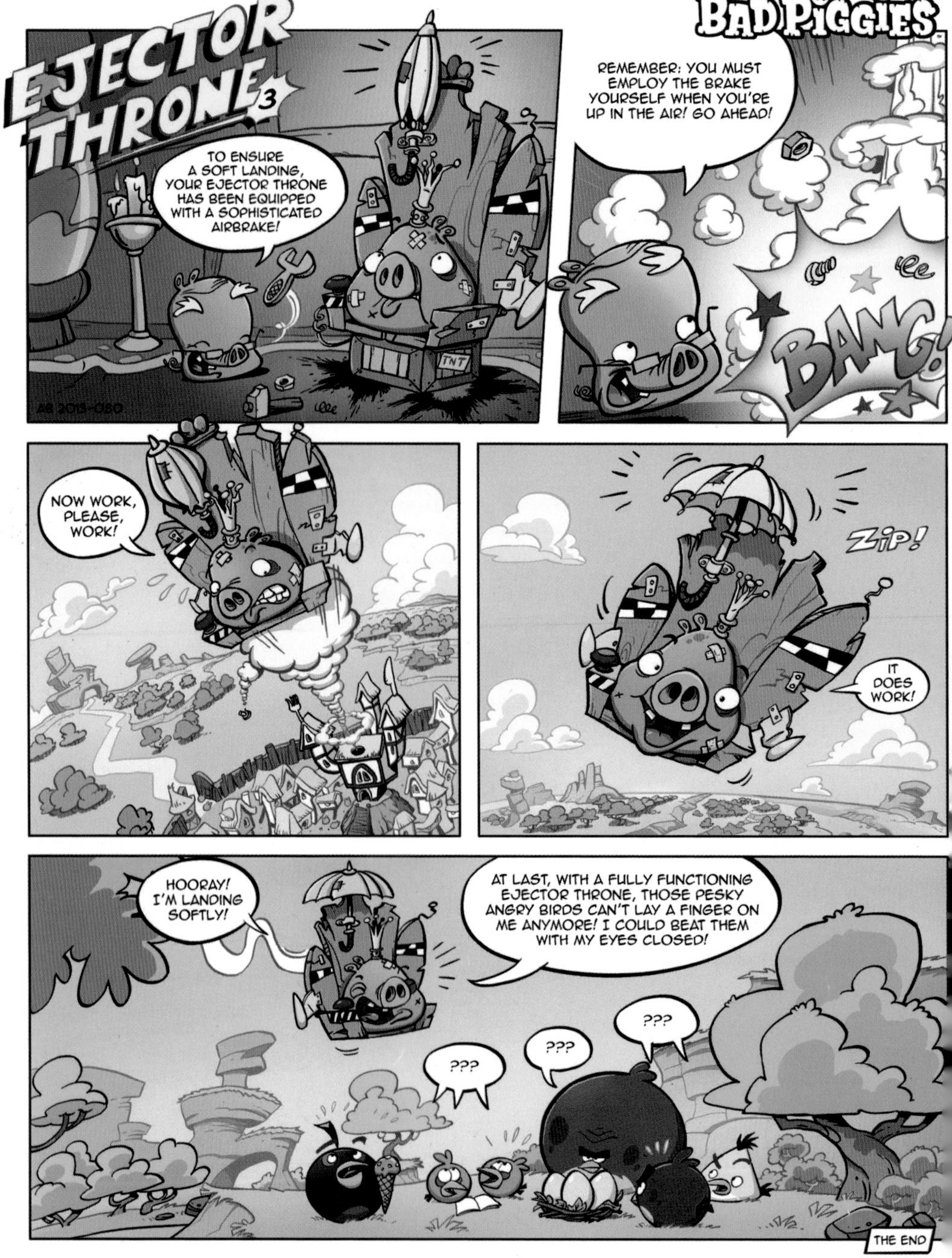

BAD PIGGIES

EJECTOR THRONE 3

TO ENSURE A SOFT LANDING, YOUR EJECTOR THRONE HAS BEEN EQUIPPED WITH A SOPHISTICATED AIRBRAKE!

TNT

AB 2013-080

REMEMBER: YOU MUST EMPLOY THE BRAKE YOURSELF WHEN YOU'RE UP IN THE AIR! GO AHEAD!

BANG!

NOW WORK, PLEASE, WORK!

ZIP!

IT DOES WORK!

HOORAY! I'M LANDING SOFTLY!

AT LAST, WITH A FULLY FUNCTIONING EJECTOR THRONE, THOSE PESKY ANGRY BIRDS CAN'T LAY A FINGER ON ME ANYMORE! I COULD BEAT THEM WITH MY EYES CLOSED!

???

???

???

THE END

WRITTEN BY: PASCAL OOST • ART AND COLORS BY: THOMAS CABELLIC • LETTERS BY: ROVIO COMICS

IDW
PACHECO
ANGRY BIRDS
COMICS
BY: JORGE PACHECO
BY: DIEGO RODRIGUEZ

Artwork by: Ciro Cangialosi

Artwork by: Paco Rodriques
Colors by: Digikore Studios

Artwork by: Ciro Cangialosi

Concept by: UPL
Artwork by: Paco Rodriques